To my grandfather, Edouard Serrigny
—G. E.

First published in the United States in 2005 by Chronicle Books LLC.

Copyright © 2003 by Albin Michel Jeunesse.
English text and translation © 2005 by Chronicle Books LLC.
Originally published in France in 2003 by Albin Michel Jeunesse
under the title *Les Métiers de A à Zèbre.*

English text design by Susan Greenwood Schroeder.
Typeset in Bokka, Stone Sans and Meta Plus.
The illustrations in this book were rendered in gouache.
Manufactured in Singapore.

Library of Congress Cataloging-in-Publication Data
Eduar, Gilles.
   Gigi and Zachary go to work : a seek-and-find game
over 300 objects to find! / by Gilles Eduar.
      p. cm.
   ISBN 0-8118-4700-4
   1. Picture puzzles—Juvenile literature. 2. Vocational
guidance—Juvenile literature. I. Title.
   GV1507.P47E38 2005
   793.73—dc22
   2004008945

Distributed in Canada by Raincoast Books
9050 Shaughnessy Street, Vancouver, British Columbia V6P 6E5

10 9 8 7 6 5 4 3 2 1

Chronicle Books LLC
85 Second Street, San Francisco, California 94105

www.chroniclekids.com

GIGI AND ZACHARY
Go to Work

A Seek-and-Find Game

By Gilles Eduar

chronicle books · san francisco

Rules of the Game

Gigi the giraffe and Zachary the zebra are off on another adventure. This time, they're on the hunt for the perfect career. From teachers to doctors to editors to astronauts, there's a whole world of work to explore. And along the way they spot plenty of fun foods, tools, buildings, boats, animals and much more. It's up to you to match the words to the pictures! Don't worry if you can't find everything, because Gigi and Zachary have put the answers in the back of the book.

From school to the boardwalk, from the mall to the space center, you're off on another grand adventure with Gigi and Zachary. Find out where this new journey takes them.

Spending a day at school

balance beam • book • classroom • climbing rope • globe • gym teacher • gymnasium • librarian • library • map •
playground • playground monitor • principal • principal's office • school secretary • slide • staircase • storyteller •
table • teacher • teacher's aide • trapeze

Reading at the book publisher's

book binder • book salesman • bookstore • computer • copywriter • customer • design department • editor • editorial department • graphic designer • illustrator • laptop • marker • paint • paintbrushes • press operator • printing press • printing room • receptionist • store owner

Filling up at the service station

ucket • gas attendant • gas can • gas pump • hydraulic lift • jack • mechanic • motorcycle courier • tire • tow truck • ow truck operator • traffic cone • truck driver • vending machine • window washer • wrench

Reviewing plans at the construction site

architect • blueprint • carpenter • chisel • construction worker • crane • crane operator • electrician • hammer • hoe • andscaper • light switch • mason • paintbrush • paint bucket • painter • plumber • pulley • overalls • roofer • saw • crewdriver • tile • trowel • upholsterer • upholstery • windowpane

Checking into the hotel

ell • bellhop • breakfast cart • bucket • chambermaid • clothes basket • counter • doorman • entertainer • fruit drink •
otel room • housekeeper • jukebox • lounge chair • masseuse • mini-refrigerator • parking valet • puppet • reception desk •
eceptionist • room keys • spa • suitcase • switchboard operator • television • terrace • thermostat • vacuum cleaner

Sunbathing at the beach

beach umbrella • bicycle • bicyclist • bucket • diver • diving mask • fish • fisherman • fishing pole • flippers • fruit vendor • ice-cream bar • ice-cream customer • ice-cream vendor • lifeguard • life ring • marine biologist • pilot • rake • sailboat • sailor • shovel • sinking ship • snorkel • sunscreen lotion • surfer • windsurfer

Browsing the shops

crobat • artist • baker • bakery • billboard hanger • bread peel • brick oven • candied apple • clown • cobbler •
obbler's form • easel • furniture maker • juggler • ladder • mail carrier • pavilion • produce stand • produce vendor •
otter • pottery wheel • salesman • sanitation worker • scale • street sweeper

Visiting at the hospital

anesthesiologist • baby • cast • dentist • doctor • florist • incubator • IV • laboratory • lab technician • maternity ward • microscope • nurse • obstetrician • operating room • scale • stethoscope • surgeon • surgical assistant • test tube • waiting room • wheelchair

Shopping at the supermarket

utcher • cashier • cash register • delivery person • fishmonger • forklift • janitor • knives • pastry chef • stock clerk • tockroom • shopping cart • turnstile

Picnicking in the countryside

apple box • apple picker • bee • bee house • beekeeper • boots • chainsaw • farmer • forest • forest ranger • hunter • ogs • lumberjack • orchard • picnic basket • rabbit • rock climber • sheep • sheepdog • sheep shearer • shepherd • pelunker • tractor • veterinarian

Launching a rocket at the space center

antenna • astronaut • astronomer • control panel operator • control tower • engine • engineer • helmet • rocket • scientist • security guard • spacesuit • telescope

Helping at the scene of an accident

amera operator • firefighter • fire hose • helmet • paramedic • patient • police officer • reporter • stretcher •
raffic guard • tunnel

Dining at an outdoor restaurant

Dressing up at the salon and fashion studio

ressmaker • fan • fashion designer • fashion studio • fountain • hairdresser • light crewman • makeup artist • manicurist •
nannequin • measuring tape • mirror • model • photographer • pin cushion • salon • seamstress • sewing machine •
cissors • spotlight • stepladder

Rehearsing at the theater

assist • cellist • chorus • conductor • costume designer • director • extras • orchestra pit • set • set designer • sheet music • spotlight • stage • stagehand • stage manager • trombonist • usher

Off on another journey

conductor • engineer • locomotive • luggage cart • newsstand • passenger • passenger car • platform • porter • souvenir shop • souvenir vendor • station manager • station master • taxi driver • ticket clerk • train track

Spending a day at school

1. balance beam
2. book
3. classroom
4. climbing rope
5. globe
6. gym teacher
7. gymnasium
8. librarian
9. library
10. map
11. playground
12. playground monitor
13. principal
14. principal's office
15. school secretary
16. slide
17. staircase
18. storyteller
19. table
20. teacher
21. teacher's aide
22. trapeze

Reading at the book publisher's

1. book binder
2. book salesman
3. bookstore
4. computer
5. copywriter
6. customer
7. design department
8. editor
9. editorial department
10. graphic designer
11. illustrator
12. laptop
13. marker
14. paint
15. paintbrushes
16. press operator
17. printing press
18. printing room
19. receptionist
20. store owner

Filling up at the service station

1. bucket
2. gas attendant
3. gas can
4. gas pump
5. hydraulic lift
6. jack
7. mechanic
8. motorcycle courier
9. tire
10. tow truck
11. tow truck operator
12. traffic cone
13. truck driver
14. vending machine
15. window washer
16. wrench

Reviewing plans at the construction site

1. architect	15. paint bucket
2. blueprint	16. painter
3. carpenter	17. plumber
4. chisel	18. pulley
5. construction worker	19. overalls
6. crane	20. roofer
7. crane operator	21. saw
8. electrician	22. screwdriver
9. hammer	23. tile
10. hoe	24. trowel
11. landscaper	25. upholsterer
12. light switch	26. upholstery
13. mason	27. windowpane
14. paintbrush	

Checking into the hotel

1. bell	15. masseuse
2. bellhop	16. mini-refrigerator
3. breakfast cart	17. parking valet
4. bucket	18. puppet
5. chambermaid	19. reception desk
6. clothes basket	20. receptionist
7. counter	21. room keys
8. doorman	22. spa
9. entertainer	23. suitcase
10. fruit drink	24. switchboard operator
11. hotel room	25. television
12. housekeeper	26. terrace
13. jukebox	27. thermostat
14. lounge chair	28. vacuum cleaner

Sunbathing at the beach

1. beach umbrella	15. lifeguard
2. bicycle	16. life ring
3. bicyclist	17. marine biologist
4. bucket	18. pilot
5. diver	19. rake
6. diving mask	20. sailboat
7. fish	21. sailor
8. fisherman	22. shovel
9. fishing pole	23. sinking ship
10. flippers	24. snorkel
11. fruit vendor	25. sunscreen lotion
12. ice-cream bar	26. surfer
13. ice-cream customer	27. windsurfer
14. ice-cream vendor	

Browsing the shops

1. acrobat
2. artist
3. baker
4. bakery
5. billboard hanger
6. bread peel
7. brick oven
8. candied apple
9. clown
10. cobbler
11. cobbler's form
12. easel
13. furniture maker
14. juggler
15. ladder
16. mail carrier
17. pavilion
18. produce stand
19. produce vendor
20. potter
21. pottery wheel
22. salesman
23. sanitation worker
24. scale
25. street sweeper

Visiting at the hospital

1. anesthesiologist
2. baby
3. cast
4. dentist
5. doctor
6. florist
7. incubator
8. IV
9. laboratory
10. lab technician
11. maternity ward
12. microscope
13. nurse
14. obstetrician
15. operating room
16. scale
17. stethoscope
18. surgeon
19. surgical assistant
20. test tube
21. waiting room
22. wheelchair

Shopping at the supermarket

1. butcher
2. cashier
3. cash register
4. delivery person
5. fishmonger
6. forklift
7. janitor
8. knives
9. pastry chef
10. stock clerk
11. stockroom
12. shopping cart
13. turnstile

1. apple box
2. apple picker
3. bee
4. bee house
5. beekeeper
6. boots
7. chainsaw
8. farmer
9. forest
10. forest ranger
11. hunter
12. logs
13. lumberjack
14. orchard
15. picnic basket
16. rabbit
17. rock climber
18. sheep
19. sheepdog
20. sheep shearer
21. shepherd
22. spelunker
23. tractor
24. veterinarian

Launching a rocket at the space center

1. antenna
2. astronaut
3. astronomer
4. control panel operator
5. control tower
6. engine
7. engineer
8. helmet
9. rocket
10. scientist
11. security guard
12. spacesuit
13. telescope

Helping at the scene of an accident

1. camera operator
2. firefighter
3. fire hose
4. helmet
5. paramedic
6. patient
7. police officer
8. reporter
9. stretcher
10. traffic guard
11. tunnel

Dining at an outdoor restaurant

1. bartender
2. busboy
3. chef
4. chef's hat
5. corkscrew
6. dining room
7. dishes
8. dishwasher
9. high chair
10. ice bucket
11. kitchen
12. maitre d'
13. menu
14. pizza chef
15. pizza oven
16. pool
17. rotisserie
18. waiter

Dressing up at the salon and fashion studio

1. dressmaker
2. fan
3. fashion designer
4. fashion studio
5. fountain
6. hairdresser
7. light crewman
8. makeup artist
9. manicurist
10. mannequin
11. measuring tape
12. mirror
13. model
14. photographer
15. pin cushion
16. salon
17. seamstress
18. sewing machine
19. scissors
20. spotlight
21. stepladder

Rehearsing at the theater

1. bassist
2. cellist
3. chorus
4. conductor
5. costume designer
6. director
7. extras
8. orchestra pit
9. set
10. set designer
11. sheet music
12. spotlight
13. stage
14. stagehand
15. stage manager
16. trombonist
17. usher

Off on another journey

1. conductor
2. engineer
3. locomotive
4. luggage cart
5. newsstand
6. passenger
7. passenger car
8. platform
9. porter
10. souvenir shop
11. souvenir vendor
12. station manager
13. station master
14. taxi driver
15. ticket clerk
16. train track